UNDER THE

FOSTER FREAK TREE

Kelley Hicken

KING
and
CASTLE

Under the Foster Freak Tree

Copyright © 2018 Kelley Hicken

King and Castle Publishing LLC

Meridian, Idaho, USA

ISBN: 978-1-949778-01-4

Library of Congress Control Number: 201891057

For N.

Different story, same love.

CHAPTER

ONE

SEFINA

I don't hate Colton Jacobs, but I wish I did. It's hard to hate a boy who donated his sixteenth birthday presents to foster kids. What I hate is the fact that he knows I got his mp3 player because his moron parents engraved his initials on it. Who does that? Parents who care, I guess. Parents who don't abandon their kids.

He knows I have it, but he pretends he hasn't noticed. It's obnoxious. He sits two rows behind me in algebra, and every single time I peek back at him, he smiles at me. I look back as little as possible. Obviously.

I shove the earbuds into my ears and thumb the letters "C.J." on the back. The engraving is so fine I can't feel the lines. I don't turn the power on because I don't have any songs loaded. But when Kasey

Taggert raises her hand and says, "Mr. Williams? Sefina is distracting me with her music again," I pretend the imaginary song is so loud I can't hear her.

He loosens his tie and sighs so dramatically that his chin rubs against his chest. A couple of girls giggle, but he ignores them. Then, he motions for Kasey to go to the back of the room instead of demanding I put the device away. He's cool to me because I get the best grades in the class. Math is easy. It has perfect, consistent answers that always make sense no matter how complicated the equation gets. Math is also the last class of the day, which turns my stomach in knots. I don't want to go back to my "not home" home.

Kasey gathers her papers and slings her backpack over her shoulder, making sure it whacks me in the side of the head. "Later, Foster Freak."

I slump in my chair and watch her saunter away from the corner of my eye. Her floral dress swirls around her thighs as she weaves through the desks. Her blond waves bounce across the back of her neck. I tug at a wisp of black hair and try to tuck it behind my ear, but it's too short and springs back up. I cut my hair by myself last week. I know that's not the best idea, but my foster parents were too lazy to get permission from my caseworker to take me to the salon. It's a stupid foster care rule. But, I'll never forget how my foster mom's face turned plum purple when she saw how I chopped it. That was, as my caseworker put it, "the nail in the coffin" for my time at the Bartletts' house, and what prompted the emergency move to the Anderson's. The only problem is now I'm separated from my little brothers.

Talk about an overreaction. I don't see why cutting my hair is such a big deal. I mean, maybe it was impulsive, but it's *my* hair. And let's face it--I will never look anything like Kasey and her eighty-dollar haircut, new clothes, and perky... everything. Why try?

Colton is watching Kasey, too, and his neck turns bright red when she sits close enough to push her thigh up against his. My chest feels like a deflating balloon. Maybe I hate him after all.

I scan my gray sweatpants and baggy white tee shirt. It's always like this when I switch families. Most of my stuff is in a black trash bag until I get around to unpacking. If I get around to it. New foster parents are always so eager to get me sent off to school that they don't notice I'm still in pajamas, or they don't care. Their own kids would never get away with it, but I always do. I can do whatever I want those first couple of weeks. That is, until the caseworker teaches them how to boss me around, like it's in her job description or something.

The bell rings, and I freeze in place. No. Not yet.

Mr. Williams shouts over the scraping of chair legs across the linoleum. I absolutely detest that sound. "If you haven't finished the chapter twenty-four review yet, you know what your homework is."

I stay rooted in place until the chatter from the boys and obnoxious giggles of Kasey's groupies are out of earshot. When I'm the only student remaining, I close my textbook and slide it into my backpack, which is starting to fall apart. Nothing that a little duct tape won't fix. I keep it around because my actual mom bought it for me. It's one thing that is legitimately mine.

"I'm so glad you get to stay at Crest Ridge," Mr. Williams says.

I stare at his pink button-up shirt that can barely contain his round belly. "Yep," I say, not sure how else to respond.

"That's pretty nice of your new foster parents to drive you all the way out here every day. What are you, two school boundary zones away now?"

I shrug. "They get mileage reimbursement, so it's no big deal."

"Well, they don't get reimbursed for their time. It's a kind service they are doing to make sure you don't have to switch schools again."

Oh, great. Do I look like I'm aching for a lecture about how sweet my foster parents are? "It's just temporary anyway, so..." I lift my eyes to meet his gaze.

He shakes his head, and I'm not sure why he looks so disappointed.

"You should really do something about how loudly the chairs scrape across the floor."

He blinks and gives me a weak smile. "I'll keep that in mind. Have a good weekend, Sefina."

Ugh, the weekend. I'm queasy at the thought of two uninterrupted days with the new foster family. I mumble my thanks on the way out the door and slip into the current of bodies, backpacks, legs, and so many different kinds of shoes, all nicer than mine. A pair of pink Converse sneakers blocks my path and I smile.

"You ditched me at lunch," Chloe says, her round face scrunched up into mock anger. She's the main reason I want to stay at Crest Ridge High, even if she hugs me too much.

I duck her embrace by "accidentally" dropping the pen in my hands. "I had to do a retake in English Lit," I say.

"Ew, that sucks. But at least you didn't have to watch Johnny friggin' hork down a bottle of milk stuffed with Hot Cheetos."

I pretend to gag. "Ugh! Are you kidding me?"

She wiggles an eyebrow. "He's kinda cute when he's being an idiot." She links her arm around mine and skips down the hall. We look ridiculous--she's bouncing like a ball on a paddle, and I'm the knot underneath that keeps her from flying away. I want to be like her someday. It's not like she has a perfect life, but she always stays happy... which can get annoying.

We make it to our lockers, and I sneer when I see mine has been zip-tied shut. Again.

Chloe groans and digs into her backpack. "Those stupid idiots. I swear, Sef, you should tell the principal about this. You know it's Kasey." She whips out her nail clippers and cuts the zip tie. She's always prepared to save me.

"Thanks," I mumble. But there's no way I'm talking to the principal about anything. All adults ever want me to do it talk, and it doesn't help anything. I turn the combination lock, pull up the latch, and open my locker. My heart sinks when I see what's inside.

CHAPTER

TWO

JEN

"What do you mean, Sefina's gone?" Michael says.

I pull the phone away from my ear and bang it against my forehead, tempted to chuck it across the school parking lot. I take a deep breath and shove the frustration down. I press the phone to my ear. "Brock got held up at school, and then I got stuck in traffic." I throw one hand in the air. "It's my fault. I was late. When I finally got here, Sefina started sobbing. She refused to get in the car. She just... took off."

"You didn't follow her?"

"Of course not," I snap. I close my eyes and lower my voice, remembering none of this is my husband's fault. "Brock and Brynn are in the car. I can't just leave them alone. I was hoping you--"

"Of course," he says. "I'll close up here and be there in five minutes."

I tap the phone onto the palm of my hand and look at my kids through the rear window. Even when only seeing the back of their heads, I can tell that Brock is bored and Brynn is talking non-stop, her blond pigtails bobbing with emphasis.

I start a text message to Sefina's caseworker.

Hi, Diane. Sefina ran off after school. I'm going to look for her. I'll let you know when I find her.

I delete it and attempt a more lighthearted approach.

Have you ever fired a foster parent two days in?

No, that's implying I've done something terrible. I turn the phone off, deciding to wait to notify Diane only if I can't find Sefina. The last thing I want is to get her in trouble again.

"Good afternoon," a male voice says from behind me. I spin to see the principal open his trunk and shove a cardboard box inside.

"Oh! Mr. Stevens, my husband will be here in just a couple of minutes. Will you please stay with my kids until he gets here?" The words rush out of my mouth before I have time to consider them. He looks at the kids and opens his mouth to protest, but I don't give him the chance before I bolt in the direction Sefina ran.

Alpine Oaks Park stretches out behind the school, next to a busy road. I run on the black asphalt walkway that winds through the maple trees. A cold breeze whips some fallen leaves into an upward spiral of orange and brown in front of me. I go right through it, startling a squirrel, who scurries up a tree.

9

I stop to catch my breath. The shaved ice stand is closed for the season. The playground is filled with young Caucasian kids, no Polynesian teenage girls hanging around. She could be anywhere.

Panic seeps in. I don't know her well enough to predict what she's thinking. I don't know who her friends are if she decides to go to one of their houses for refuge. For all I know, she could have arranged to meet with an older boyfriend who picked her up, and they are on their way to Las Vegas.

Tears well in my eyes, and I squeeze them shut, letting their warmth trickle down my cold cheeks. I mutter a quick prayer and will myself to think like a fifteen-year-old girl who has lost everything that matters to her. It's impossible. I can't imagine what she's feeling. I turn in place, scanning the ground for anything, footprints in the leaves or... I spot a crumpled piece of paper a few yards away. It's bright white and dry, which means it is a new deposit on the wet, rotting leaves. I pick it up and straighten it out. My heart freezes when I read what it says.

"Hey Loser. If I was your mom I'd get wasted and leave you too."

My face burns when I see another piece of paper a few feet away. Then another and another.

"Stay away from Colton. You are nothing but a FREAK!"

"Can't you just go away already? Your family doesn't want you, and neither do we."

"Sefina is dumb. That's all."

I stop reading them, my pulse racing so fast that I can hear the blood rushing in my ears. I pick up paper after paper until my hands are filled with the hateful words. How could anyone be this cruel? If I ever find out who wrote these... I fantasize about putting the little brats

10

in a chokehold. Then my ears tune in to a sweet singing that chimes above the nearby traffic noise and playground squeals.

I put my palm to my heart when I see Sefina sitting with her back against a maple tree. She is swimming in a sea of fallen red leaves, belting out the words to Simon and Garfunkel's "Cecilia." What a strange song choice for her age. Her voice is perfect, strong, stunning. I could stand there all day listening to her, but my concern for her wins out. I go to her. Her hands are over her ears, and her eyes are shut. Her face is streaked with wet trails. Her confident voice completely contradicts her wilted posture.

I drop the papers to the ground and bend down to place my hand on her knee.

She stops singing and stares at me with dark-brown eyes, so different from my kids' blue eyes.

"I'm sorry," she says automatically.

What do you do for a girl who has watched her dad die? How can a girl who's seen such a thing, and then watched her mother spiral into drug addiction, still be singing? And then these bullies, these selfish little monsters...

What was I thinking taking in a teenager? I have no experience with anyone over seven years old. Who am I to help her, when I already know she is far stronger than I could ever be? At this moment, I can't think of anything to say, so I just scoot next to her and hug her. She is so much bigger than my kids, sturdier, and her hair smells like coconut.

Sefina hugs me back for a moment and then releases me. But I just squeeze tighter. After a second, her arms come back around me, and I feel her breath hitch. "You have every right to cry, sweetheart," I murmur, unable to stop my own tears. She starts to sob. I don't know how long we sit like this, but eventually, she pulls back and wipes her face with the inside of her shabby tee shirt. I wonder if she has anything nicer to wear, or if she enjoys clothes shopping at all.

"This is my favorite tree," she says.

"A maple tree?"

"No." She sniffs and rubs her eyes. "Well, yes, but I mean this specific tree."

I look up through the half-naked branches against a sleepy gray sky. I run my hand over the rough ripples of bark. It's no different than any other maple tree.

"If you sit here, it blocks the wind." She points to the long slope on the other side of the tree. "It's a nice view of Mt. Timpanogos and the stream." I follow her gaze from the snow-tipped mountain down to the irrigation ditch that runs under a small red bridge. "And there." She points to the right. "Across the street. See the little yellow house with green trim? I used to live there with my grandma and little brothers." The red brick stairs are crumbling, the paint is fading, and what's left of the brown lawn is covered in weeds. "It looked better when Grandma owned it," Sefina says, as if she can read my mind.

"You must have a lot of memories attached to that house."

She plays with her shoelaces. "She taught me how to bake butterscotch cookies and macaroons."

I take that opening. "Would you teach me how?"

It's like an invisible wall shoots up between us. "I don't remember the recipe."

"Oh, okay," I say, not sure what just happened. "These notes," I say, gesturing to the crumpled heap of paper on the ground. "This is completely unacceptable. Who wrote them?"

Sefina shrugs and grabs her pink canvas bag. There's a hole in the bottom corner, and I make a mental note to buy her a new backpack. She turns it upside down and dumps out the contents. At least another dozen notes come tumbling out. "They stuffed my locker with them."

"Who did?" I ask, somewhat relieved to see she hasn't bothered to open any more notes. "We can do something about this. We can make sure this doesn't happen again. You have a right to feel safe at school."

She shakes her head. "I'm not sure who did it, and I don't want to know. These"--she throws a fistful of the notes into the air--"are nothing compared to the rest of my problems. So what if I'm just a foster freak to them. It doesn't matter."

I watch her for a moment, trying to form the right words. When they don't come, I ask, "If the notes didn't bother you, why did you run away? Did something else happen?"

She pulls her knees to her chest and hugs them, unable to meet my gaze. "You'll think I'm stupid."

"No. No, I promise I won't."

She hesitates. "I just didn't want to get in your car. It's too..."

I wait, but when she won't answer, I push. "It's too what, sweetheart?"

"Scary."

I shake my head, not understanding. "But this morning...

13

Michael drove you to school."

She nods, "Yeah, in a big ol' Suburban. It's not like..." She buries her face behind her knees.

Understanding blooms. "It's not like the car your family was in the day of the accident." She holds her breath and tenses.

"You feel safer in the Suburban?" Her black hair bobs up and down twice. "Okay, then. We'll work it out, all right?" I don't know how I can fit one more thing into my schedule, but somehow, I'll have to figure out how to trade cars with Michael each school day after he's done hauling his morning loads. "He should be at the school by now. Let's see if he'll give you a ride home, okay?"

She lays her head sideways on her arm. "Can you drive me instead? In the Suburban?"

I squeeze her around the shoulders and smile. "Of course."

Her smile comes slowly, hesitantly, but it comes.

CHAPTER
THREE

SEFINA

"So…Sefina," Dr. Swenson says in her breathless, let's-get-this-over-with voice. She shuts the office door and plops her hunched old form into her swivel chair. The cushion releases air like her rear end is choking the life out of it. That's what therapists are good for, I guess. "One moment, dear." She puts on the glasses that dangle from a chain around her neck. She pulls open a file drawer full of numbered white binders and grabs 9.19.0302, which is me. It's probably the name she calls me when she goes home to her perfect, mentally healthy family and talks about her day.

I rearrange my legs on the sofa. It's pretty comfortable because it's old and broken in. The black leather has faded to brown and is cracked where all her patients sit. The armrest is in really bad shape, but that's partially my fault. There is a small hole with yellow foam that pokes out. Every time I come, I peel a bit more leather away, opening that wound wider.

Dr. Swenson flips through the notes in my binder. Her lips move as she reads, which makes me want to throw the nearby box of tissues at her. Instead, I close my eyes and try to ignore the buzzing of fluorescent lights, the ticking of the black and white wall clock, the muffled sobbing from the office in the next room.

"Okey dokey," she says, closing the binder and tossing it to the desk. She pulls her glasses off and gives me a sort of sneer that must be her attempt at a smile. "You've had a bit of a shake-up, I hear. You've changed foster families again?"

I nod and look away.

"Can you tell me about how that's going for you?

I slink down in my seat, putting my knees between me and her nosy questions. "It's fine," I mumble.

"Do you understand why you were removed from the Bartletts' home?"

I know exactly why. I refused to listen or obey their stupid rules. If Charlene told me to wash the dishes, I would shatter them. If she told me to turn the music down, I would blast it, hoping her ears would bleed. Once, Sean gave me money to buy new shoes, and I bought a sweater instead. He made me return it. I can name tons of reasons why they kicked me out, but all I say to Dr. Swenson is, "Because they are idiots and never wanted me to begin with."

If this annoys her, she doesn't show it. "How about the Andersons? What do you think about them?"

I shrug. "I've only known them for a couple of days."

"And?" she pushes.

"I guess they're okay so far." Except I am very Samoan, with brown skin and black hair, while they are all very white and very blond except for Jen, who has reddish-brown hair. Plus, the kids are too young. Brynn is six and in that super-annoying princess stage. Brock is ten and just plays video games all the time. I don't really know Michael yet and it's weird to hang out with an adult man, so I stay far away from him. But all I say is, "Jen seems nice."

She smiles again. "I'm glad to hear it. I think she's nice, too. I've worked with some of their previous foster kids before, and they've always been supportive parents. I hope you come to trust Jen enough to confide in her."

I roll my eyes, but she doesn't react. Man, I hate that about her.

"Have you had any contact with your brothers since the separation?"

"No," I say automatically. Of course not. Nobody asked me if they could stay with the Bartletts. Nobody suggested they move out with me. Why couldn't we all go to the Andersons together?

"And how do you feel about that?"

Seriously? She's really asking me that? So, I do what I always do whenever she asks obvious questions just to get me talking: I say, "I don't know."

She narrows her eyes and scoots her chair a little closer, making the wheels squeak across the plastic floor mat that protects the horrific forest-green Berber carpet. "What is good about your brothers staying with the Bartletts?"

"I don't know," I mumble. But I think, The Bartletts are nice to them. They get three meals a day, they aren't watching Mom spiral down into drug addiction, they aren't watching Grandma lose her mind to dementia. Someone is taking care of them.

"What is bad about it?"

"I don't know," I say, but I know the answer so clearly it aches. The person taking care of Tane and Ku is not me. It's not me that tucks them in at night. I mean, do the Bartletts know that Tane loves fruit but gets rashes when he eats strawberries, or that Ku likes to read his Daniel Tiger book while he's still dripping from his bath, wrapped in a towel cocoon before he's dried off and in pajamas? Do they know that both boys used to be scared of the dark but that I told them how monsters are attracted to light, like moths, so now they bravely turn their lights off every night?

"You seem worried," Dr. Stenson says. "Would I be correct to assume you are concerned about your brothers?"

I say nothing.

Her eyebrows scrunch together. "Sefina." Her tone is drenched with disappointment. At least it's a reaction.

I stare back at her, daring her to say one more word. She shakes her head and turns toward her desk, opening my binder to take notes. I pick at the hole on the armrest, trying to drown out the sound of her pen scratching across the page. Stubborn. Refuses to talk. Damaged. Unworthy of my time and attention. She could be writing anything on that stupid page.

"Why don't they want me, too?" I blurt out. When Dr. Swenson turns toward me with eyes wide, I cover mine with the palms of my hands. "I could try again. What is so wrong with me?"

"Is that what you think?" she asks, "that something is wrong

18

with you?"

I groan and clench my fists in front of my eyes.

"Perhaps the Bartletts feel too inexperienced to handle a teenager. Did you ever consider that?"

I don't respond.

"Maybe they worry they're not good enough parents for you. Sometimes, foster parents just want to keep the birth order of their kids intact. The point is, their decision might not have anything to do with you."

I let out a shaky breath. "We were supposed to stay together," I whisper, not trusting my voice to get any louder. "My caseworker said we'd stay together."

Dr. Swenson nods. "Change is difficult for everyone, Sefina, and you've had an awful lot of change in your life."

I wipe away the last of my tears and take a deep breath, realizing again that Dr. Swenson cannot do anything to help me. She can't cure Grandma of dementia or make Mom come back to get me. She can't reverse the Bartletts' decision to send me away. All Dr. Swenson can do is babysit me for an hour and make my caseworker and my new foster parents feel like they can check therapy off their list of things to do today.

Well...check. I'm done.

When Dr. Swenson decides I'm really not going to say anything else, she tells me my homework is to confide my feelings in someone else. I think about that longer than I want to. Who would I talk to? Jen or Michael? No way. Chloe? I can't imagine dragging any more of my issues into that friendship and tainting her opinion of me. Grandma is too out of it to even know who I am if I called the nursing home. No, I don't need to confide in anyone. I'm on my own.

CHAPTER

FOUR

SEFINA

The Andersons' house is the only single-level house in a tightly packed subdivision on the side of Traverse Mountain. I could touch both their house and the neighbors' at the same time. It looks tiny compared to the rest of the mansions in the neighborhood, but it's kind of cute. It's mostly covered with gingerbread-brown stucco, while the lower half of the house and the column near the front door have light-brown and gray stonework. The front door is a faded teal color that matches the window boxes. The bushes in front are a fiery red, and even though the neighbors' yards are beginning to yellow, the Andersons' lawn is as green as spring.

Jen drives the Suburban up the sloped driveway and pulls into the garage. Their cat, the meanest little feline I've ever met, scurries outside. But when I get out and shut the car door, she hurries back in.

Maybe she's decided it's too cold to hunt right now. After all, the sun has begun to set, and the clouds are close and look full of ice.

"Mommy! Mommy! You're back!" Brynn bounds down the steps from inside and crashes into Jen, who steadies herself against the car. She bends down and kisses the top of Brynn's head. I don't know why something small and stupid like that makes me jealous, but it does a little.

"Phew!" Jen swipes the air under her nose. "You've been cooking onions, haven't you?"

Brynn moans. "It's the only thing Daddy lets me do!"

I follow them into the house, through the messy laundry room, and down the hall, past my baby-pink room on the right and Brynn's purple room on the left. At Jen and Michael's closed bedroom door, we swing left into the family room, which connects to the kitchen. Brock is in front of the huge TV, playing a video game, drowning out the Christmas music playing softly in the background with his whoops and frantic button pushing. Michael is behind the kitchen island, wearing a cartoony Santa-and-reindeer apron and dropping some raw hamburger into a pan of sautéed onions.

"Ah ha! The whole family is here," he says with a huge grin. "Just in time for tacos."

Jen drops her purse and phone on the sofa and then makes her way over to Michael, hugging him from behind. She looks exhausted and much older than him as he joyfully whistles "Silver Bells" over the steaming pan of meat.

"You do know it's far too early for Christmas, right?" she says, still hugging him.

"Well, it feels like Christmas to me." He looks up at me and winks. "Look at this beautiful gift we've been given."

Jen smiles at me, too, but I don't know if I should smile back. I'm not sure what the weird feeling is in my stomach. Am I feeling flattered? Annoyed? No. Hungry. I'm definitely feeling hungry.

"Yeah," Brynn says. "She's almost as good as a baby!"

I frown, not understanding. "Huh?"

She smacks her forehead. "Oh, I forgot to tell you! Mommy's baby died in her tummy. She was a girl like you!"

I look to Jen, who is obviously in shock at her daughter's admission. "Brynn, why don't you join your brother?"

Brynn shrugs and skips over to the TV, grabbing the nearest controller.

"I can set the table," I say, looking for a way out of this awkward moment.

"Thanks," Jen says. "I'll get you some cups to fill."

I wait near the kitchen table, noticing three picture frames hung on the dining wall between two large windows. Two of the frames have recent school pictures of Brynn and Brock. The third frame has nothing but a big question mark in it. What's that all about?

JEN

I set out five glasses, and Sefina quietly fills them with water at the fridge and sets them on the table. Meanwhile, I go to the dish cabinet and pull out a stack of plates. I grimace, remembering that I have exactly four plates because, last year, I had a decluttering phase and got rid of everything extra. I set the dishes back into the cabinet and head to the pantry for the stack of paper plates. I hate washing dishes anyway, so this will make for an easy cleanup.

But when I hand the five paper plates and five napkins to Sefina, she freezes, staring at them. "What's wrong?" I ask, but she just shakes her head and carries them to the table. I never know what's going to set her off into a sad memory. I can't predict anything. I know nothing about this girl in front of me.

"We're ready!" Michael booms so that Brynn and Brock will hear and turn off the game that has engrossed them. When all of the steaming food is piled onto the table, Brock and Brynn sit in their usual seats. Sefina pulls out the metal folding chair I brought up from the basement, but Michael grabs it from her. "Nuh-uh." He wags a finger at her and motions her to sit in his own seat. "I do not allow my girls to sit upon un-cushioned chairs."

A shy grin blooms on Sefina's face, and I can't help but smile at my sweet husband. Brynn snorts a laugh while Brock hastily jumps up, pulls the cushion from his chair, and puts it on top of Sefina's chair. "Double cushions for the princess." He bows, and though he looks like a complete nerd, I'm so proud of him I could burst.

We all giggle, even Sefina, as she sits atop her throne, heads above where Michael sits slumped in the folding chair.

I'm dying to ask her how the meeting with Dr. Swenson went, but between Brynn and Brock, there is no getting any conversation in that expands beyond Minecraft or the latest My Little Pony movie. Sefina is quiet. She picks at her food, and I wonder if it doesn't taste good to her. Maybe it's too different from what she's used to. Or maybe she's depressed. I assure her that she doesn't have to finish it all if she's not hungry, and Brock volunteers to eat what she doesn't want. She seems relieved to hand the taco over to him.

"Do you like ice cream?" I ask.

She nods, and the other kids jump up and down in their seats, yelling in celebration. "I have some in the outside freezer. I'll get it while you guys clean up your plates."

When I finally get the back door open, I'm juggling four different kinds of ice cream in my arms. I nearly drop them when Sefina pushes past me in the hallway and slams her bedroom door behind her. I hurry to the kitchen and set the ice cream on the counter. Michael has his arm wrapped around Brock and is talking quietly to him. Brock puts his head down on the table, and I can tell from the set of his shoulders that he is moping.

"What happened? I was only gone for thirty seconds!"

"Brock made Sefina mad," Brynn chirps. "She washed her paper plate!" She laughs like it's the funniest thing.

"She what?" I say, not understanding.

Michael sighs. "We just had a brief moment of insensitivity. He didn't mean to upset her. Sefina tried to wash her paper plate, and Brock teased her for not just throwing it away."

"Oh." I think of how she froze when I handed her the plates. Surely, she'd used paper plates before. Right?

"Can I go say sorry?" Brock mumbles, his face still on the table.

"Let me talk to her first." I go to the cupboard to pull out a real bowl. I scoop each kind of ice cream in it and make my way to her room, armed with a spoon and no idea where to begin a conversation with her.

I knock lightly. "Sefina? It's Jen. Can I come in?"

After a second, I hear the squeak of her bed and footsteps. The lock clicks, and she opens the door. She immediately crawls back into her bed.

Although I'd like to close the door behind me so we can speak privately, I leave it open so that she doesn't feel trapped or threatened. "Apparently, Brock needs a little coaching in manners. I'm sorry he upset you," I say.

"It's okay. It's not his fault."

As I approach and hand her the bowl of ice cream, she scoots over. "You can sit down," she says.

I sit and watch as she takes the first few bites. I rack my brain for anything to say. Nothing comes.

"My grandma didn't have any real plates," she says. "We would sometimes have plastic plates that we would wash. She'd get so mad if we threw them away."

I nod, my heart clenching. "You are more resourceful than I knew! And if you want to reuse paper plates here, you can. If you want to throw them away, you can do that, too. Now that we know, we won't pass judgment on you."

She swirls her spoon between the chocolate and strawberry scoops. "Can I ask you a question?"

"Of course you can."

She hesitates, glancing up to meet my gaze only for a second. "This room. Was it supposed to be for your baby?"

I smile even though that familiar sadness fills my body. "Yes, at one point. That was a long time ago, though, and I'm happy you are here to fill the space."

"Are you still sad?"

I play with a loose yarn on the bed quilt. "I suppose I am still sad, in a way. There is no time limit for grief. It ebbs and flows however it wants, and I'm perfectly willing to experience it all." I watch her contemplate that thought, and then add, "If you'd like to redecorate, you know, to match your personality, we can do that."

Her left eyebrow quirks up. "Really?"

"Of course! You should make it your own."

She thinks about that for a minute, and then she hands me her bowl, not even halfway finished. "Is it okay if I go to bed now?"

"Absolutely. Do you want the light off or on?"

"Off."

She quickly hugs me. "Thanks, Jen."

"Goodnight, sweetie," I say, surprised at the spontaneous affection. I flip off her light and shut her door behind me. Michael and the kids are involved in a rousing game of Monopoly as I rinse out her bowl and put it in the dishwasher.

"Jen?" Sefina calls from the hallway.

I turn around, worried at the panic on her face.

"Can you stay with me? Just until I fall asleep?"

CHAPTER

FIVE

SEFINA

I nearly laugh out loud when I walk into Mr. Williams's last-period class and see he has placed sliced tennis balls on the foot of every chair leg in the room. I hear several mumbles of confusion, but I know exactly why he's done it. I pull my chair out, and it slides silently across the linoleum.

Mr. Williams smiles at me and taps one finger to the side of his head. I agree. It's a great solution to that horrible sound.

Kasey flops down in the seat next to me, sending a cloud of her flowery scent my way. She huffs as she takes in the sight of my outfit. Her eyes land on my hair, and she scowls. Then she turns to her other side and whispers to Beth loud enough for me to hear, "We should have included hygiene tips in those notes we gave her."

Beth giggles, and I feel my face grow hot. Instead of sitting when the late bell rings, I head to the door and grab the hallway pass. I figure Mr. Williams won't get mad at me for using the bathroom if I'm quick. I just need a minute to calm down before I spend an entire period next to that stuck-up hag.

On the way out the door, I shove it a little too hard, and it hits someone on the other side.

"Ow!" Colton rubs his shoulder and smiles crookedly at me. "Hi, Sefina."

I want to apologize and make sure he's okay, but I hear Kasey snort behind me, so I just push past him without saying anything. Like a jerk.

"Hey," he says, following after me. "I put something in your locker for you."

I freeze and spin toward him. "Excuse me?" I would never have guessed he was part of Kasey's cruel prank.

He takes a step backward, obviously shocked by the venom in my voice.

I shove him against the classroom door. "What is your problem? Why are you and your girlfriend such jerks?" I know I'm yelling loud enough for the whole class to hear because, as I look through the window in the door, all eyes are wide and on me. Mr. Williams makes his way past the desks and to the door. He pulls it open just as I shove Colton again. Colton stumbles backward and lands on his rear end, right on Mr. Williams's shoes.

"Whoa, there, Sefina!" Mr. Williams chides. "I think it's time we had a chat."

"Ooooh," the class whistles behind him, some people laughing and some shaking their heads like I am their greatest disappointment.

I stalk out, hearing the clatter of Mr. Williams's footsteps following behind. Fine. If he wants to talk, I'll give him something to talk about. I stop in front of my locker and twirl the combination lock.

"What in the world just happened?" he says, his hands on his hips and his face red. "I can't imagine Colton would have done anything to warrant that kind of treatment."

"He's a bully," I say. "They're all bullies. Last week, they filled my locker with notes." The words tumble so fast out of my mouth that I lose my voice in a shaky breath. I finally yank the locker open and see it. The note from Colton is crisp, white, and folded, just like the rest of them. I hand it over to Mr. Williams and slide my back down the lockers until I land on the floor.

I close my eyes and hug my knees while he opens the paper and begins to read. I hear the paper fold again, and he grunts as he plops down on the floor next to me.

"So…help me understand. Have you told Colton that you're not interested in dating him, and he keeps pestering you?"

I lift my head up and give him what I hope is my most appalled expression. "What? No! He's never asked me out."

He smiles and shakes the note in the air. "Are you sure?"

I yank it out of his hand and nearly rip it as I try to get it open.

Dear Sefina,

We don't really know each other, but I think you're incredibly smart and I like how nice you are to everyone around you. Okay, and you're pretty, too. I was wondering if you'd like to hang out sometime?

30

I look at his phone number, written in unfamiliar, blocky handwriting, and gasp. "Oh no," I whisper. "Oh no, oh no! I'm such a friggin' moron!" I pound the note against my head.

Mr. Williams chuckles, and I jump because I've already forgotten he was there. "Not what you expected?"

I shake my head and try not to cry. "Oh my gosh, I pushed him down in front of everyone."

"First of all, it wasn't everyone. Second of all, I'm sure if you explain… you know, be honest, he'll understand your earlier reaction."

I bang the back of my head against the locker a couple of times.

"Now, what about the notes that were in your locker last week? Who is harassing you, Sefina?"

I let my head hang between my knees while I try to think of an excuse to not tell him about Kasey and Beth. Then I see it—the dark-red stain at the crotch of my jeans, and I'm horrified.

JEN

"I can't believe I forgot to get her tampons," I say, pulling down the bedspread and climbing in. "Of course she starts her period the very week we get her. Gah!" I grab my head and squeeze. "She won't answer when I knock."

"She probably can't hear you over all that singing," Michael mumbles around the toothbrush in his mouth.

It's eight o'clock, and Sefina hasn't come out of her room since I picked her up from the nurse's office and brought her home. She turned on her music and has been singing ever since. Loudly. She didn't even come out for dinner.

I don't worry too much about her starving because, as I was doing laundry earlier this morning, I noticed she has stockpiled her closet with things from the pantry. A loaf of bread, a big jar of peanut butter, honey, and a family-sized bag of potato chips. I would never let my younger kids get away with that, and I had planned on talking to her about it after school, but then the nurse called.

I groan and cover my eyes with the crook of my elbow. "She must be mortified. She's already being picked on at school, and then this happens. Why can't she catch a break?"

I hear Michael spit and rinse his mouth. The bathroom light switch clicks, and the bed shakes as he hops on. "She'll be fine," he says reassuringly. "And it's not your fault. She could have told you she needed tampons. Besides, maybe nobody even noticed."

I snort. Sometimes, his positivity is obnoxious. "With her luck, whoever wrote those horrible notes saw and made a huge deal about it."

"Have you talked to anyone about those notes yet?"

I scoot back on the bed, arranging the pillows so I can sit up. "No. She didn't want me to. I'm worried I'll just make things worse." I shake my head. "I don't know. What should I do?"

Michael shrugs and sucks air through his teeth. "I think you should tell someone whether she wants you to or not. She has a right to feel safe going to school."

I nod to be agreeable, but I'm not sure I can go against Sefina's wishes. Is it more important for the bullies to be reprimanded or for her to be able to trust me? I don't know the answer, but I know it's not coming to me tonight, so I pull the cord on my lamp and settle into the darkness.

A few hours later, I wake to the quiet shuffling of Sefina arranging a makeshift bed on the floor next to me. When she gets comfortable, I can barely see moonlight reflecting off her eyes as she stares up toward the ceiling. I reach out my hand, and she takes it and closes her eyes. The surge of love and concern I feel toward this stranger's child feels like it may burst out of my chest. I close my eyes, too, letting the tears soak into my pillow.

CHAPTER

SIX

SEFINA

The Good Ol' Times Ice Cream Parlor is buzzing with little kids getting their sugar highs. I like little kids. I like how they can smear mint ice cream all over their hands and face and don't care who sees it. In their eyes, the bigger the sticky mustache, the better. I can't help but smile at a little girl who carefully pokes at a fake giant spider that dangles from a cotton web in the window. It's like she knows it's fake but has to check, just in case.

The Halloween decorations feel out of place in a parlor that has pink vinyl chairs with heart-shaped backs made of coiled wire. The walls are bubble-gum pink, as are the tabletops. Even the employees wear pink-polka-dotted aprons.

I swivel on the barstool, which creaks under my weight. I still can't believe I'm hanging out with Colton Jacobs. How did he talk me into this again? Oh, yeah. Relentless text messaging. And by text messaging, I mean printed text in my locker because my life is lame and I'm not allowed to have a cell phone. Thanks again, Diane Stewart, caseworker extraordicrappy.

Colton is leaning over the counter, pointing at the menu while a husky blond waitress nods in approval. I'm not listening to their conversation. I'm too busy trying to figure out why she has a tattoo of Batman holding a cross on her lower back. It peeks out over her belt every time she reaches forward to wipe the counter.

I'm close to quizzing her about it when Colton elbows me. "Cotton candy, huh?" He grins. "What are you, five years old?"

I snort. "So sorry. I didn't realize there are maturity levels to ice cream flavors."

"Sure! If you're really, really, outstandingly old, vanilla is the only option. A step down from there is butter pecan. You know, before the dentures give out and won't handle nuts anymore."

I roll my eyes but can't help smiling.

Why am I here? Why did he ask me out?

The waitress comes back with two cones. She serves me first. "Here you go, hon. Cotton candy single scoop. And a double-scoop, double-loaded bubble gum with rainbow sprinkles for the gentleman."

I laugh so loud it makes him jump, but his cheeks turn a little rosy, and I want to take it back.

"Don't mock it till you try it." He holds the cone out to me. "Have the first bite."

I trade him cones and motion for him to try mine, too. "Oh, mmhmm," he moans, and then he shakes his head. "Remind me to get this next time we come here."

I hide my smile behind his cone and then take a small bite, trying to avoid getting an actual chunk of bubble gum in my mouth, which is difficult. It's good but suspiciously sweet. Like Colton.

We trade back, and I say, "I'm kind of an ice cream expert. You should always follow my lead."

"Good to know," he says.

I lick the blue and pink ice cream, turning the cone to catch all the drips. The sweetness blooms on my tongue, and I'm transported to another day. The last day of normal.

Dad had taste-tested all of our cones, calling it the "Dad tax." He always did that—always taking what seemed like a bigger bite than his mouth was capable of holding. Then he'd do his deep belly laugh while we all complained about what a pig he was. Mom shook her head with a quiet smile. She looked like me except her hair was straighter and her skin was not as dark. And she had those black freckles that I'm still jealous of.

Maybe it was the sugar, or maybe I hadn't had enough sleep the night before, but I remember being absolutely enraged at my brothers. We must have been exceptionally rude because Mom threw away our cones before we were done and piled us back into the car to go home. We were so close to home it should have only taken three minutes to get there.

In the back seat, Ku pulled a strand of hair from my head and then tickled my ear with it. I slapped his hands away three, maybe four times before I screamed at him to stop. Dad shushed me from the driver's seat. Ku tried again, moving slow, like a snake, as if I wouldn't notice him if he held his breath. Tane snickered next to him, waiting for the payoff. The second that stray hair touched my ear, I jammed my elbow into his side. The air gushed out of his lungs, and he moaned.

Dad turned away from the steering wheel with the angriest look I'd ever seen on his face. Then Mom screamed. The windshield shattered into a million pieces. We were hanging upside down, and the radio was still playing, "It's gonna be a bright, sunshiny day…" I smelled smoke and turned my head. Dad was in a heap on the ground. It didn't make sense, being upside down, looking at Dad's unmoving body. It was like magic. A second ago, he had been in the car. How had he done it?

"Sefina?"

I shake my head and stare up at Colton. He's worried. I follow his gaze to my hand. It's freezing and sticky with pieces of crushed cone littering the table underneath. I stare at it, wondering when I managed to make such a mess.

Colton pulls a stack of napkins from the holder at our table and carefully takes what's left of the ice cream cone out of my shaking hand. He doesn't say anything. What could he say? I am a total freak. He's probably mortified to be seen with me.

"I'll uh…" I stand up abruptly. "I need to wash my hands."

I leave the mess sitting there on the table and run to the bathroom. Even the stalls are pink, with rainbow-colored polka dots everywhere. The cold tap feels warm to my freezing hand. I'm afraid to look up at the mirror, but when I do, I'm relieved that I haven't been crying. I guess that's progress. One less thing to be embarrassed about.

I dry my hands with a paper towel and wonder if I can sneak out without Colton seeing me. We could just pretend like this never happened, but I know that would be rude. Grandma would smack the back of my head for losing my courage. So, I steady my breath and step back into the shop.

I'm a little surprised that Colton is still here. I sit back in my seat.

"Sorry," I mumble. "I just…" I can't think of what to say.

He pushes a fresh scoop of cotton candy ice cream in front of me.

"I figured cones are not your friends today, so I opted for a nice, safe bowl and spoon."

I force a smile, rubbing my hands together between my knees. "You didn't need—"

"I wanted to!" Colton says. "I mean, I don't want a little freak-out moment to spoil our first date."

I roll my eyes. "This is not a date."

He grins, and I try to shake off the fact that he's turning my stomach in knots.

"But you admit that you had a freak-out moment?" he teases. "Was it something I said?"

I hesitate and then shake my head. "No. It's not you at all."

He watches me, waiting for more of an explanation. I want to throw up a wall between us, but Dr. Swenson's homework assignment keeps rattling through my brain. My palms begin to sweat. I reach for the purple spoon from the bowl in front of me and mindlessly stab the scoop of ice cream. "It's funny, you know," I say, trying not to look directly at him. "Strange what things bring back memories."

He nods. "Like how every time I smell peaches, I think about canning them for days at my aunt's house one summer."

"Exactly," I say. "I guess the ice cream reminded me of some stuff."

He leans both arms on the table and looks at me so directly that I cannot help but look him in the eyes. "Tell me about it," he says quietly. It's not a demand, though. He seems genuinely interested in what I have to say. Not to diagnose me. Not to tell me how to deal with my problems. Just to get to know who I am.

I can't talk about the accident. I just can't. Not without ugly crying, and I do not want to go there in front of Colton. So, I tell him how Mom, my brothers, and I were in the hospital a really long time. I skip the part about how I found out Dad had died, and go straight to how Mom never came back. Not really. I tell him Grandma took us in when Mom went to rehab for painkiller addiction. I also tell him about Grandma getting so sick that she'd call me "Mama" and beg me to sing her a lullaby. I might as well have been her mom because I took care of her and my brothers for a long time.

I don't even mind when the tears stream down my face. He doesn't mind either; he just moves closer. When I'm done, my bowl of ice cream is completely melted, and Colton Jacobs's hand is on mine.

"Wow." He exhales and leans back in his chair. "How are you still standing?"

I pull my hand away. "Don't act like I'm something special. Anybody would have done the same if their mom had abandoned them."

"So, that's what you think," he says, the kindness gone from his eyes. "That she abandoned you?"

"She did," I say. "She loved her drugs more than her kids."

That shake of his head, that look of disappointment… Oh, man, how I want to slap it off his face. How dare he judge me after I just bared my soul to him? My nostrils flare, and I push away from the table, standing up so fast that the chair tips over behind me. "You don't know anything about it, Colton."

He puts his hands up in surrender. "All I'm saying is you deserve a break. And maybe your mom does, too."

His words sink down to my gut like I swallowed lead bullets.

"Forgiveness is the best move, Sefina. You work through problems, not avoid them, or nothing will ever get better."

Even as I say the words, I know they are wrong. So wrong. But I can't stop them. "I will never forgive her. And I will never forget how you've made me feel." I turn and take two steps before stopping and pulling the mp3 player out of my pocket. I slam it on the table in front of him, ridiculously disappointed it doesn't shatter into a million pieces. "I don't need your judgment, I don't need your pity, and I don't need you."

And just like that, Colton Jacobs is out of my life.

CHAPTER
SEVEN

SEFINA

Dr. Swenson tilts her head and smiles at me. She's a little too elated that I followed through with my homework assignment for once. "How did that feel?" she asks.

I shrug because I can't remember exactly how I felt. It's been over a month. I do know that I'm not exactly happy I spilled my guts to the cutest boy in school. We hadn't spoken to each other since before Halloween and it is almost Christmas, now. I hate that I miss him. I barely know him. I fold in on myself, sure that I've made a huge mistake. Dr. Swenson, of course, notices my posture sag.

"Hold on there," she says, her eyebrows pinching together. "What are you feeling right now?"

I pick at the yellow fluff coming from the hole in the armchair. I want to ignore her like I always do, but Colton's words come back to mind. Work through the problem, not around it. Otherwise, nothing will change. And I want everything to change.

I take a deep breath and sit up a little taller. "It was good at first to have somebody to talk to." I don't want to get into details of my blowup with Colton, so I scramble to change the subject. "And...I've been thinking about it a lot. I think figured something out."

She raises an eyebrow. "Good. Would you care to share?"

"I shouldn't blame Mom for leaving me anymore. She didn't prescribe herself those pills. She didn't mean to get addicted. She didn't cause the accident." I look straight into her eyes even though I can't see her through my tears. The words fall out of my mouth so fast I can't stop them. "I caused the accident. It's my fault Dad is dead. It's my fault Mom had to use the painkillers. It's my fault I couldn't take good enough care of everybody and we got put in foster care. It's my fault the Bartletts didn't want me. And now I've lost my brothers and my parents and—"

"Hold on." Dr. Swenson holds her hand up. "None of this is your fault, okay? None of it." She scoots her chair closer to me and leans her elbows on her knees. She's so close I can smell her old-lady soap. "Every event that happens in life is the culmination of many events leading up to it. You might have distracted your dad while he was driving. I don't know. But he chose to take his attention off the road. Your mom chose to make you leave the ice cream shop early. Your brother decided to pester you. The other driver...who knows what decisions they made to get them in that spot at that moment. On any other day, at any other moment, those decisions would have turned out just fine. It's nobody's fault. There is no blame to place."

46

I put my face in my hands. I hope she's right. "But if I hadn't been angry at the ice cream shop, and if I hadn't been angry in the car…"

"If, if, if!" Dr. Swenson grabs my hand and gently pulls it away from my face. "The 'if' game will get you nowhere, Sefina."

I squeeze my eyes tight to push the tears away. The room is silent except for the buzzing fluorescent lights overhead and the ticking clock. I focus on that. Nothing but the tick, tick, buzz.

"I'm proud of you." I hear her chair roll back towards the desk.

I look up, surprised.

"I'm really, really proud of you for opening up."

I don't bother to keep the contempt out of my laugh. "Why? Talking doesn't help me feel any better. It just makes everything worse. Why does everybody want me to talk about it?"

"You said it helped to talk to Colton."

I snort. "At first. Then he…" I wave my hand away. "Freaked out."

There's that stupid head tilt again that she uses to show she's interested.

"I don't know why I told him. I should have chosen someone else. Chloe, maybe. She wouldn't think I'm…" I stop, looking for the right word. "Crazy," is what most people would say.

My favorite thing about Dr. Swenson, and maybe the only thing I actually like about her, is that she doesn't put words in my mouth. She waits.

"Too dramatic," I finish.

She nods slowly and opens her mouth to say something, but

then she shakes her head. "Do you think you are too dramatic?"

I shake my head.

"Did your friend accuse you of being too dramatic?"

I pause and then shake my head again. "Not exactly."

"How did he react?"

I remember standing there like a brain-dead zombie, crushing my ice cream cone like a friggin' psychopath. Dang it! What if he told Kasey what a freak I am? "He was cool," I say, sinking back down. "And then judgy. It doesn't matter. He'll never ask me out again." I want to throw a blanket over my head and die, but Dr. Swenson would have too much to poke at if I tried.

"Give it time," she says. "And maybe give him some credit. It's hard to know the right thing to say to someone who is grieving."

I scowl and listen as she gives me my next assignment, which is to continue talking to the people around me and to write my feelings in a journal. She even gives me a pink notebook and sparkly purple gel pen. As if telling my story in glittery letters will make it less horrible. I throw it in the trash on my way out the door.

CHAPTER
EIGHT

JEN

I turn the Suburban's radio down, but Sefina immediately turns it back up. I try again with the same result. Finally, I just turn it off altogether.

She turns and scowls at me as if I just ran over her favorite dog.

"It's fine," I say. "You don't have to tell me about therapy, but you don't need to cover the silence with noise. I need to be able to focus on the road."

The way her face falls…oh man, did I really just blame her for distracting me as a driver? I curse myself inwardly, and the car falls deadly silent. Unable to stand it any longer, I say, "Hey, you never told me what happened between you and Colton. Is everything okay?"

No response except for her sinking deeper into her seat. Oops again. Time for a change of subject.

"I need to stop by the store. Is there anything special you want for dinner?"

Silence.

When I look at her, I see she is staring out the window at the cemetery. Or, maybe she's watching the first few flakes of snow spiral to the ground. Her chest is puffed up, and she's not breathing. Why is she holding her breath? Once we pass the cemetery, she lets all of her breath out. Strange. My curiosity gets the best of me. I turn on my blinker and enter the suicide lane. I make a U-turn and head back to the cemetery.

Again, she holds her breath, and she doesn't release it until we have passed the last headstone. I turn the vehicle around again. This time, Sefina looks at me in confusion. "What are you doing?" she hisses.

I don't say anything. I just accelerate faster until we're back to the cemetery, and she sucks her breath in again. This time, I turn onto the narrow road between headstones and drive as slowly as possible.

Sefina puffs out her cheeks and shakes her hands. I smile at her, and she breaks out into laughter. "What are you doing to me?" she yells.

"Why in the world are you holding your breath?"

She smacks her hand on her head. "Because I can breathe, but the dead can't, and it makes them jealous. Me and my brothers always hold our breath when we go past a cemetery." She pounds a fist on her leg. "Great. You made me breathe. Now the spirits are going to haunt me."

She says this, but I can see by the humor in her eyes that she

50

doesn't really believe it.

"Oh dear," I tease. "Whatever can we do to appease these poor souls?" I stop the car on the narrow road and turn to her.

Her expression tightens. "Sing to them." Abruptly, she unbuckles and bursts out of the Suburban door. At the top of her lungs, she sings, "Somewhere over the rainbow, way up high…" Her breath explodes in white puffs in the cold air.

I wait in the car in awe at how she's twisting the notes into a minor key. Her voice is haunting, evocative, and it's obvious she is alone at this moment. I don't exist. The cemetery doesn't exist. It's like she's closing her eyes and pouring her soul into the void. Every note is strong and clear. Goosebumps shiver down my arm.

"Birds fly over the rainbow, why then, oh why can't I?" she finishes. Her chest heaves with the effort, and she just stands there, almost as if she's forgotten where she is. After a moment, she gets back in the car as if nothing happened.

I blink hard and shut my gaping mouth. "Wow!" is all I can say.

She smiles, but I see where the tears have trailed down her cheeks.

I put one hand on my chest and one hand on her shoulder. "Wow."

She giggles at my reaction.

"Sef… Sefina! You are incredible!"

She shrugs. "Everybody in my family sings. It always makes us feel better." She looks out the window, wringing her hands for a minute. When I can't do anything but stare at her, she turns back to me. "Are we just going to sit here all day?"

I shake my head, but it takes me a minute to turn the ignition. My mind is swirling with possibilities of voice lessons, music theory classes…music therapy.

"Do you ever write your own songs?" I ask.

She shakes her head.

"Well, that's a shame," I say, pulling back onto the main road. "Because I would sure love to hear what Sefina Nafo has to say."

She automatically reaches for the power button on the radio. Then she stops herself.

I let out an exaggerated groan and say, "Fine, but keep it low."

She sings like nobody is listening the rest of the way home. When we pull onto our street, I see the maroon Honda CRV that belongs to Diane Young, Sefina's caseworker. My heart skips a beat. Sefina must have seen it, too, because she stops singing. When we pull into the driveway, Diane steps out of her car.

"Did you call her?" Sefina says, the accusation thick in her tone.

"No," I say. "This is definitely unscheduled."

SEFINA

Diane sent me to my room so she could talk to Jen privately. Does she have the tiniest clue how humiliating that is? I don't need to be babied—I can handle whatever needs to be said. I fling myself onto the bed and curl the pillow around my face and ears, screaming as loud as I can. Then I throw the stupid thing onto the ground, sending piles of paper flying off my desk.

I need to know what they're talking about. If it's about me, I have a right to know, don't I? Tiptoeing to the door, I turn the handle as silently as I can. I slip out of the room and sneak down the hallway until I can hear their muffled voices. Deciding they must be all the way in the front room, I slink past Brynn, who is lounging on the couch, ripping into one of her unicorn sticker books. When she looks up at me, I put my finger to my lips to shush her from giving me away. Her little eyebrows squish together, but then she quickly loses interest in me.

"Longer than we had anticipated," I hear Diane say.

"So, what are we talking here? Another month? Two months?" Jen asks.

There's a pause, and then Diane says, "Natia hasn't done as well as we had hoped."

I flinch at my mom's name.

"She hasn't met any of her objectives as ordered. At this point, both Natia and the judge are leaning toward terminating parental rights."

"No. No, no, no," I whisper. She can't give up. She can't! She just needs to see us, remember how much she loves us…

"What does that mean? For Sefina? For the boys?" Jen asks.

Diane clears her throat. "The gold standard in this situation, of course, would be to find a family that would adopt all three children together. It is, however, highly unlikely. The Bartletts have offered to adopt Tane and Ku, and if no other family steps up, we will probably go that direction and try to find a permanent home for Sefina, separate from her brothers."

I can't listen to it anymore. My head is pounding with so much anger, so much hurt. I hurry back to my room and shut the door. Suddenly, the room feels suffocating. I fling open the window and knock out the screen, sticking my head out and taking huge gulps of crisp air.

I have to get out of here. I need to find Mom and tell her that giving up is not an option. She needs to fight for my brothers. She needs to fight for me. Isn't that the most basic instinct of a mother? She's just forgotten because she's not around us.

I look around the baby-pink room and find my canvas bag. It won't take me long to pack.

CHAPTER

NINE

SEFINA

I knock on the door to Grandma's old house, shivering from a blast of wind that flicks snow into my face. It has probably taken me over three hours to walk here from the Andersons' house. I'd have a better idea if I was allowed to have a stupid cell phone. The sun is mostly gone, and my nose, fingers, and toes are all numb.

I hear footsteps from inside, and the porch light clicks on. The inside door creaks open. I can't see the person standing there because the light flooding around them makes them look like nothing but a dark shadow. "Can I help you?" a deep male voice asks.

For a second, I think about turning around and forgetting this whole idea. But I gather up my courage and say, "I um... I used to live here, and I left something in a closet. I was wondering if I could come in and get it really quick?"

"There was nothing left that I know of."

"It was hidden in the door, between the metal and the cardboard lining. You wouldn't have seen it unless you knew where to look. Please?"

The man thinks for a moment, and then he pushes the screen door toward me. "Alright, I suppose you can take a look."

I step inside and get my first glance at the man. He's wearing a red-checkered flannel shirt and dingy jeans. His feet are bare, and his face is covered with stubble. "Thanks," I mumble, stopping short in the entryway.

Everything is so achingly familiar and different at the same time. The furniture is all different. Where grandma had color splashed everywhere, this guy has every shade of brown imaginable. It smells like cigarettes and a litter box now. But the kitchen looks exactly the same, with the yellow floral border at the top of the walls and the ancient pea-green stovetop with the dent in the front where Ku hit it with a baseball. Even the wall where Grandma used to measure our heights is still marked with our initials.

I swallow down a lump of emotion and point to the hallway. "It's this way."

The man follows me, which makes me nervous. I wonder if there is anyone else here, as I am leading a strange man into a bedroom all alone. I look around for anything I can use as a weapon, just in case, and see there is a beer bottle on a desk in what used to be my old bedroom. I look over my shoulder, but the man just leans against the door frame instead of coming in. I draw a deep breath through my nose and turn to the closet.

Two yellowed, metal bi-fold doors sit slightly ajar in front of me. With some effort, I shove the left one open and step inside. On the other side of the door, I move the cardboard insert up to reveal a yellow Post-it Note stuck to the inside.

Spring Lake Drug Rehab and Addiction Center

1453 N Mapleton St

Santaquin

I show the back of the note to the man and quickly stick it in my pocket. "Thank you," I say. "That's all I needed."

"You all alone?" he asks.

My stomach turns in knots. Lie, Sefina. "No, my uncle is outside waiting for me." I walk toward him, and he backs into the hallway, letting me pass.

"Hey," he says. I stop, wondering if I should just run out the door as fast as I can. "I have half a pizza left that I'm not gonna eat. Why don't you and your uncle take it? It will keep you warm. There's a storm coming."

As if on cue, my stomach growls. I think of the jar of peanut butter and half a loaf of bread I have in my bag, and I know that won't last me too long. "Sure," I say nervously. "My uncle loves a good pizza."

He nods, and something in his eyes tells me he doesn't believe I have an uncle outside. Still, he heads to the fridge. He sets the still-warm box in my hands, and I almost moan at its effect on my icy fingers.

"Take care now," he says as he opens the door for me.

"Thank you."

I step outside and take a deep breath as the door shuts behind me. I'm okay. I'm safe. I have Mom's last-known address and a free dinner. Not bad! But as I'm about to head over to the park to dig into the pizza, I catch a flicker of light from the front window. The man is watching me through his window blinds. I pretend to wave at someone down the street and yell, "Uncle! I have pizza!" I run down the street until I know I'm out of his view. Then I take an alternate route to my tree. Settling in under the bare branches, I'm happy that the slope gives me some protection from the cold breeze. I try to remember how long ago Mom first entered rehab. Years ago. What if she didn't go back to the same rehab she was in when I lived with Grandma? I snuck the original address from Diane's binder. She would have killed me had she found out. And it's probably all for nothing because, if Mom chose a different rehab center, I will never find her.

I shove a piece of pizza in my mouth. How am I going to find her without getting caught? Most importantly, what am I going to say to my mother when I finally see her?

I shake off the fact that I'm alone and have nowhere to keep myself warm from the coming storm. I wonder how Jen is reacting. She must know I'm gone by now. I left my door locked and stereo on, though, so unless she went outside and saw the open window, maybe she doesn't know. I close my eyes, trying to ignore the cold ache blooming in my chest when I think about Jen and Michael. No, they are better off without me. They know it, too; otherwise, Jen wouldn't have been asking how much longer they have to house me. I can still hear her asking, "So, what are we talking here? Another month? Two months?"

I'm nearly done scarfing down the pepperoni feast when I see a cop car pull up at Grandma's old house. I sink down low to watch, grateful that there are no park lamps nearby.

An officer gets out the squad car and approaches the front door. When the scruffy man answers, the cop takes notes. After a minute or two, the man points in the direction I went after leaving his house. The officer gets back in his car and goes the same way.

I don't know if the guy suspects I am a runaway or if he reported me as a thief. Either way, I am guessing that cop will eventually sweep the park and find me. I need to get out of here, hopefully to someplace warm. I finish up the last piece of pizza and then sit on the box. It gives me a little separation from the cold ground so I can actually think.

Access to a phone or computer with wi-fi would help. I could look up the phone number for Spring Lake Rehab to see if mom is there before I find my way to Santaquin, which is probably a good forty miles south. Libraries are closed. I probably can't get into the school this time of night. Breaking in is a stupid idea. I could try a coffee shop and hope that someone will let me borrow their phone. No, that would be too suspicious.

I look up, hoping to catch a glimpse of the moon. No luck. There are no more leaves on my tree, and the sky behind her is snow pink. She must be tired after nine months of blossoming, giving shade, and then dropping her leaves. I wish I could sleep the winter away with her, dead to the world for a season.

I consider going to Chloe's house, but that would never work. She lives on the second floor, and her window faces the backyard with that giant Doberman that has never liked me. The second that thing barks, Chloe's dad will investigate, and I'll be caught.

I groan, knowing where I have to go and hating it so, so much.

CHAPTER

TEN

JEN

Michael kicks his snowy shoes off on the front mat and steps over the threshold. He's holding a drink carrier with two lidded cups. He switches the carrier from hand to hand as he removes and hangs his coat, jingling the keys inside the pocket. I scowl at the fact that he is still alone. He's been gone for hours, scouring neighborhoods, looking for any trace of Sefina.

He hands me one of the cups. "Cocoa? I didn't want to come home completely empty-handed."

It feels sickeningly hot against my skin as I stare out the front window at the three inches of snow that has accumulated since midnight. The sun is rising, and so is my panic.

"We've done everything we can, Jen. We should get some sleep. Diane will let us know if she turns up."

I shake my head slowly. Although it serves as a response to my well-intentioned husband, I'm shaking my head at my own stupidity. How could I have not known she left? How could I fall for the stereo-and-lights-on trick? As it was, I didn't even consider Sefina was up to anything except ignoring my pleas to let me in—until the last time I stood knocking and felt a cold breeze from under her door wash over my bare toes. I knew the window was open and her belongings were gone before I ever unlocked the door.

"Hours," I whispered. "I lost hours when I could have been looking for her. And with every minute that passes, the search radius gets bigger and bigger." My voice cracks at the end of that sentence.

I feel the cushion dip underneath me as Michael takes a seat. "It's not your fault," he says.

I stand up. Then, not knowing why I stood, I sit back down again. "She's so vulnerable out there, Michael. What if someone…"

He shakes his head as if that's not even a possibility, but I see the pain in his watery eyes. "Let's not worry until we have something to worry about, okay?"

But I'm not listening. "She must have heard us talking. I thought she might be okay with us wanting to adopt her, but…" I set the cocoa on the end table and use both hands to rub my temples. "Of course, it's so much more than that. She's been here…what? A month? Just because we want her to stay doesn't mean she wants to stay."

Michael wraps an arm around my shoulder and kisses the top of my head. He smells like snow and chocolate. "Maybe she just needs time to cool down. I'm sure that when she gets hungry or cold enough, she will head home." He takes a sip.

"Home?" I say, a thought dancing in the corner of my mind. I jump off the couch so fast that Michael nearly drops his cup. "Oh my gosh, Michael! I know where she went!"

SEFINA

"Get up, Sefina," Colton hisses.

I flinch at the light as he yanks open the curtains.

"Go out the window and then knock on the front door."

I sit up, completely disoriented. His room looks so different from when I climbed in through the window last night. It seemed like a bad dream, how I came in crying and begging him to drive me to Santaquin, and he was less than happy to see me. "Do what now?"

He pulls me out of the bed by the arm and pushes me toward the window. "Just do it."

Clumsily, I climb back out of the window. It's freezing as I stumble around the side of the house through several inches of snow. I press down my frizzed hair with my fingers and check for morning breath. It's horrible, so I grab a handful of snow and shove it in my mouth. When it melts, I spit it back out, hoping that did the trick.

Oh, weird! Did I really just sleep in Colton's bed? I wipe the sleep from my eyes, remembering how he didn't even want to be near me last night. He heard me out and then told me to get some sleep and that he'd sleep on the family room couch. The last time we were together, I yelled at him. And now I'm begging for favors? Bad, bad idea.

I find my way to the front door and hesitate before knocking. What am I doing here? He did tell me to knock, though. Or was I dreaming that?

I knock.

I hear Colton yell, "I've got it," and then his footsteps pound toward me. He flings open the door. "Oh, crap!" He slaps his hand to his forehead.

I don't know what to do. Did I do something wrong? Was I not supposed to come to the door after all?"

"Who is it?" I hear a woman's voice holler from inside.

"It's Sefina, Mom. I totally forgot today is Saturday. I promised to drive her down to Santaquin today."

I sag against the door frame and let out a huge breath.

"What?" She steps into the hallway behind Colton. "Well, let her in! Don't make her stand in the cold all day."

As I step inside, she reaches out to take my hand. "Hi, Sefina! I'm so glad to finally meet you. I've heard a lot about you."

"You have?" I am surprised when she pulls me into a hug. This woman, barely taller than I am, smells like friggin' cinnamon rolls. That figures. His life is perfect.

"Yes!" She pushes back to look me over. "Oh, yup. You're just as pretty as Colton says."

I snort and look down at my shoes, which are dripping on their entry mat.

"He tells me you're living with the Andersons. Did Jen drop you off? I'd love to say hello." She stands on her tiptoes and looks outside.

My heart skips a beat. "I didn't know you knew each other." I throw an annoyed glance at Colton, but he's not looking at me. He's too busy rummaging through a desk drawer nearby. He pockets a set of car keys.

"Oh, yes. We met in foster-parent training classes a few years back. Lovely family, which I'm sure you know by now."

I nod, and an ache grows in my chest. "Yeah, they're really nice people." It takes me a second to internalize what she just said. "So, you're…a foster family?"

Her smile drops a little. "Didn't Colton tell you that?"

"No, Ma," he says. "I haven't told her my life story yet, but let me do it. You'll get the pertinent details all wrong." He kisses her on the cheek, and she laughs.

"Fine. Where did you say you're going? Come grab some breakfast to go."

I let out a shaky breath and follow them to the kitchen, where Colton's mom loads up a couple of paper plates with, of course, cinnamon rolls and scrambled eggs. I barely hear their conversation, but I know it includes warnings about slick roads, taking it slow, times we need to check in with her, and "Don't forget your coat."

And just like that, I'm standing next to Colton's silver Pontiac Grand Am, petrified, while he reaches in through the driver's side door and sets the plates of food on the dashboard. He walks around the outside of the vehicle, checking the tires.

"Uhhhm… Do you have a bigger car we could drive?"

His eyebrows draw together. "No. Why?"

Crap, crap, crap! "It's just…small."

His shoulders sag. "Are you kidding me right now? You wake me up in the middle of the night, steal my bed, force me to lie to my mom, and now you're complaining about the car I'm driving you all the way to Santaquin in for free?"

"I can pay for the gas if you—"

"Stop, Sefina." He pinches the bridge of his nose. "It's just…" He rests against the car and folds his arms across his chest. His gaze falls to my face, unflinching, accusing. "When somebody is trying to be nice to you, at least try to be gracious about it."

I know he's talking about our date at the ice cream shop. I hadn't considered that maybe he was trying to help, not judge. "You're right." I nod and then look down so he won't notice the tears forming. "I'm sorry. Thank you."

"You okay?" he asks.

"Yeah, fine." But when he steps aside and opens the passenger door, I don't get in. "Sorry, I just need a second." I shake my hands out and hop up and down. Outside of where we stand in the garage, the wind is picking up, swirling clouds of fallen snow off the driveway. I should just call Jen and ask her to bring me to Santaquin in the bigger, safer Suburban. No, she's probably so mad that they'll try to transfer me to another placement the moment they find me.

"Does your phone have wi-fi?" I ask. "Before we waste our whole day"—and possibly die in this deathtrap— "I should make sure my mom is actually there."

After Colton helps me find the browser on his cluttered screen, I look up the website for Spring Lake and call the office number listed. When the secretary confirms there is a Natia Nafo in residence, I thank her in a choked voice and hang up.

I nod to Colton. Then I suck in a deep breath and get in the car.

CHAPTER

ELEVEN

SEFINA

We inch our way down I-15 through slush and traffic. The first major snowfall always brings out the worst in Utah drivers, and the Provo area just might be the worst of it. Maybe it's the college kids trying to get to their classes on time that causes us to slink forward like four lanes of giant, metal snakes. Colton has been quiet since we pulled out of his driveway, and he asked if Jen and Michael knew what I was up to. I don't think he likes the idea of driving me outside the town limits without their permission, but he doesn't say anything about it.

"So, how many foster kids have you had in your family?" I ask, hoping to lighten the mood with easy conversation. Plus, I don't know much about Colton aside from every angle of his face that I've inspected over the past couple of years.

"Just one," he says.

I have a momentary freak out. "Are you…" I stop, wondering why I should feel bad asking this question. "Are you a foster kid?"

"No." He smiles. "My mom almost died when I was born, so she and Dad decided they were done having kids. I think it was fine until I got a little older and they thought I might be lonely."

I bit my lower lip, imagining perfect Colton Jacobs experiencing that all-too-familiar feeling. "Are you lonely?"

He shrugs. "I probably was. Reece wasn't what I expected, though. As a twelve-year-old, I was hoping we'd get a boy my age that I could play football with or video games. You know, more of a friend. But my parents ended up bringing home an eight-year-old boy with deformities and more special needs than I knew was possible for one human being."

"What was wrong with him?"

"He, uh…" Colton swallowed. "His biological mom was a heavy drug user when she was pregnant with him. We're talking meth, heroin, cocaine…the whole works. He had all kinds of problems from that. I think the biggest problem was that he had microcephaly, you know, where the head is really small."

"That's so sad," I say.

"Yeah. He looked like he was missing the back half of his head. He had some messed up organs, too. And the seizures… The seizures were really bad."

"How long did you have him? Did he go back to his family?"

Colton's left knee erupts into tapping, and he shifts in his seat. "We are his family. We adopted him. He died about a year ago after he fell and hit his head during one of those seizures."

I look away from the pain in his eyes and try to think of something comforting to say. There is nothing. Nothing. "Wow. Colton, I'm so sorry."

He rubs the bottom of his nose and looks out toward the snow-covered mountains. "You know, he wasn't the family I asked for, but holy crap, I love that kid. I mean, I'm almost relieved for him that he doesn't have to suffer anymore, but it's hard. I miss him, you know?"

The realization pulls me down like quicksand. "So, when you donated your sixteenth birthday presents to kids in foster care…" I watch as his breath hitches. "That was in honor of Reese, wasn't it?"

He nods slowly, releasing a shuttering breath.

"Oh, freak. I'm such an idiot. I'm so sorry I slammed the mp3 player on the table like that."

I hear a muffled noise and look up to see Colton trying not to laugh.

"What?" I elbow him. "Shut up!"

He full-out belly laughs now, and I fold my arms and glare at him until he gets himself under control.

"Sorry," he says. "But when I got home that day and figured out that you never put any music on the thing, I laughed all night." He laughs again. "Oh, man…all those times you pretended like you couldn't hear Kasey being a brat. And that one time you actually started dancing when she was trying so hard to make you mad." He laughed again, shaking his head. "I'll tell you, my respect level for you— poof!" He motioned like his brain was exploding.

I snorted and then laughed, too. "I can't stand that girl."

"Yeah, she's…something else," he says, getting a little quiet.

"Don't let her get to you, Sef. She's got nothing on you, and she knows it."

"You gonna try to tell me that she picks on me because she's jealous?"

"Trust me. That's exactly what's going on. That girl gets everything she wants."

"Except you," I say.

He's not smiling anymore. "Except me."

JEN

I bang on the shabby white door for the third time before a man finally answers. I have obviously woken him up, and he's not too happy about it.

"Do you not see the no soliciting sign?" he grumbles.

"I'm not…" I start to say. Then I shake my head. "I'm looking for a little girl who may have been in this neighborhood. She's Polynesian and—"

"Yeah, I saw her," he says. "I already called the police and told them everything I know." He starts the shut the door.

"Sir, please! Did she say anything about where she was going?"

He rubs his face hard, like he's still trying to wake up.

"Nah, she just wanted to grab a little piece of paper she had stashed in the closet. Looked like an address. I gave her a pizza and sent her on her way."

"Did she—"

"That's all I got for you, lady. I don't want to get involved." And with that, he shuts the door.

"She's my daughter!" I yell, hoping he will change his mind and give me one more clue as to where she went. But the door stays shut. "She's my daughter," I say again, this time just so I can hear it fall from my lips. It feels like the truest thing I've muttered in my life. No matter what any birth certificate or court document says, Sefina is my daughter.

I step backward, nearly falling off the porch and into a snowdrift. Carefully, I tread back down the steps, zipping my coat a little higher. Sefina was here. At least I know her well enough for that. I look across the street to the park, remembering that fall day, not so long ago, when she sang her frustration out under her favorite tree. I cross the street, trying to remember exactly which maple it was. I'm not good at knowing different kinds of trees, especially when all the leaves are gone, but I remember how the slope ran behind the tree, so I follow it until I find a pizza box.

I gasp and pick it up, shaking it mercilessly, hoping that some clue will magically fall out so I know where she went next. Nothing. Think, Jen! I drop the box and grab my head with both hands. There are no footprints in the snow. She must have left before the worst of the snow hit. But where?

And what did she take from her grandma's old house? If it was an address, whose was it? My hands fly to my mouth, and I squeeze my eyes shut. Of course. She's trying to find Natia.

CHAPTER
TWELVE

SEFINA

Spring Lake looks like an ordinary house from the outside. It is two stories high, with cream siding and forest-green shutters and trim. Two chimneys poke up over the snow-covered roof. There is no smoke coming from them. There is no breeze to ruffle the sleeping tree on the side of the house. There is no movement in the front parking lot or anywhere around the house. I would have wondered if I was looking at a photograph except for the gushing of water coming from the gutters as the snow melts in the afternoon sun.

The house sits on a small parcel of land that backs up to a field. I'm guessing there is a garden underneath the snow there, because it has fallen in perfect rows. I remember Grandma telling me how Mom had learned to grow peas at her rehab center. It's hard to imagine Mom here, in this place I've never seen before, carrying on life as if she had no kids. Is she happy here? How many times has she walked through that huge front door? Did she spend her summer evenings dangling her legs over the porch edge, laughing and making jokes with her new friends?

I jump when Colton touches my elbow. "Are you ready to go in?"

Am I? Am I ready to see the woman who is ready to relinquish me and my brothers? What if she looks like the same addict who left us—scarred, sunken-eyed, angry? Can I handle that?

"Yes," I say before I can psyche myself out too much.

"Wait here," he says as he climbs out the car. The jangle of keys is cut short as he shoves them in his pocket and shuts the door. He sidesteps a puddle as he scoots around the front of the car, his breath curling around his face in smoky tendrils. He opens my door and reaches a hand down to help me out. I take it, noting the difference between the top of my brown hand and his pink palm. He doesn't seem to notice, so why do I?

My face heats up as he pulls me close and hugs me. "It'll be okay, Sefina," he says softly. "And whenever you want to leave, just give my hand a squeeze, and I'll get you out of there, okay?"

"Okay." I try to smile up at him, but I can't. And when he steps to my side and takes my hand, I look at Spring Lake and gasp. It seems so much bigger when I'm out of the car.

Colton takes a step forward and then looks back in confusion when he realizes I am rooted in place.

I shake my head, tears welling.

JEN

"You have arrived," the GPS informs me as I pull into the parking lot at Spring Lake Drug Rehab and Addiction Center. My heart jumps into my throat when I see Sefina safe, standing next to Colton. I jump out of the Suburban. When the door shuts behind me, Sefina turns. As soon as she sees me, her expression goes from confused to relieved to…I don't know what. She runs to me, her arms stretched out. She nearly knocks me over, sobbing into my coat.

I hold her tight, fighting for control over my own emotions. I kiss the top of her head over and over. "You're okay. You're okay," I say. "Shh. Everything is going to be okay." But I'm not sure if that's true. Has she already seen her mom? What did that woman tell her to break her heart? I feel the anger rising, but I shove it back down, knowing it won't help Sefina.

Colton leans against his car, looking a little sheepish. I'll deal with him later.

"You scared the crap out of me, Sefina. You can't just run off like that. What were you thinking?"

"I'm sorry," she cries. Her sobs are slowing down now. "I'm sorry, I'm sorry." When her crying finally ebbs, I expect her to pull away, but she doesn't. She holds on to me like I'm tethering her to the earth.

"Did you find your mom?" I ask, dreading her response.

"No," she says, sniffing. "I got scared."

"That's okay. Do you want me to go in with you?" It feels like self-betrayal to offer, which is ridiculous. I don't get to claim dibs on

75

this girl. She has a mother. With all of the foster children I've cared for, I've never minded playing second fiddle to bio mom, but with Sefina, it's different.

When Sefina pulls away and nods, my heart sinks.

She says a quick goodbye to Colton and then slings her backpack over her shoulder and links her arm in mine.

We get to the bottom step before she halts.

"What is it? Do you need more time?" I ask.

She shakes her head. "I just wanted…" She looks at her feet for a minute. "I don't want another placement. I don't care if I never get adopted—I don't want to be put in another placement. But I know it's too late for that, so I thought if I could convince my mom that she still wants us…"

Her confused expression mirrors my own when she looks up at me. I don't know how long we stand like that before the door creaks open.

"Sefina?" a woman's voice croaks.

Sefina pulls her head back and whips her gaze to the Polynesian beauty at the door. "Mom!" She lets go of me, and I know my arms have never felt so cold.

CHAPTER

THIRTEEN

SEFINA

I'm sitting in the family waiting room between my past mom and my present mom. How science fiction is that? I stare ahead at the brick wall that has been painted maroon and shift my weight on the sofa, stealing glances at the woman I haven't seen in months. It's obvious that she is surprised that I'm here and she doesn't know what to say to me.

"Tell me everything, Sefina. What have you been up to lately?"

I should tell her about how I'm rocking my math class and that I'm thinking about joining choir next semester. I should tell her that Tane and Ku are loving their new foster family and she doesn't need to worry about them. There are hundreds of things that I should tell her, but I'm kind of pissed off that she looks so normal and healthy, so all that comes out of my mouth is, "Did you find a new man or something?"

She flinches hard. "What?"

"Or maybe you got a new job that lets you travel the world?"

She shakes her head, trying to figure out where I'm going with these questions. "No, Sefina. No man, no job. I've just been here, working through some problems."

"Because the only other reason I can think of that would make you want to give up your kids is that you hate them. Do you hate me, Mom? Because I didn't mean to get Dad killed. It was an accident, and I'm really sorry."

I feel Jen's hand on my knee right before Mom hugs me. "No, sweetheart. Don't think like that. I don't hate you or your brothers. Not at all. And I don't blame you for anything."

"I do," I say. "I distracted him. If it wasn't for me, he'd still be alive. You wouldn't have gotten addicted to the pain pills. And now you're ready to give us away forever? What about Tane and Ku? What did they do wrong?"

"Enough!" she yells, covering her ears with her hands. She stands up and paces around the room for a minute. Her hands shake as she rubs the sides of her head. I know this look. She's in withdrawal, which means she's in no position to hear me or help me feel better. What was I thinking?

"I'm sorry, Momma." I stand up and tug on her arm, leading her to the couch. "Come sit down."

She obeys and flops down next to me. She slumps over and lays her head in my lap. "It's so hard, Sefina. You know? It's so hard to get off these drugs and to do it all alone." She starts sobbing, and there's nothing I can do but stroke her hair and murmur that she'll be okay.

Jen looks angry, which I can't figure out. She has no right to judge, but I'm sure I'll hear her opinions later. Or sooner from the look on her face. I clench my fists when she starts in on me. "Even if it was a hundred percent your fault, which it is not, how long do you think your dad would stay mad at you for causing an accident?"

I shake my head and try to refocus my attention on my sobbing mother.

"Really, Sefina. How long would he stay mad at you?"

I refuse to answer her, though I know she's right—Dad wouldn't have stayed mad for more than a minute. He wasn't like that. I stare down at my mom. Looking at her is like looking in a mirror that has aged me thirty years. Except for the freckles, which still make me a little jealous.

Jen scoots closer and forces my chin up. "You are a child, Sefina. A child! You don't have to bear all this weight on your shoulders. You should be taken care of, not acting as the caretaker."

I slap her hand away from my shoulder. "This is none of your business! Why are you even here?"

"Okay, all right now," Mom says as she sits up and positions herself between me and Jen, which is completely unnecessary because Jen gets up and storms out the door.

I growl and throw a cushion across the room.

"Hey! Respect the house, young lady," Mom says.

"She's just so…" I can't think of a word to describe Jen.

Mom turns to me, and for once, her gaze is steady. "She's just so right. It's not fair to you kids to make you put your childhood on

79

hold while I get my act together. I want you to be free and feel safe so you can enjoy your life. I'm not planning on leaving you forever. I'm always gonna be your momma, okay?" Tears slip down her cheek. "I'll always, always, always be your momma, but I can't take care of you three on my own. I'm not strong enough yet, and I don't know when, or if, I ever will be."

I bend toward her and put my forehead to hers. "I miss you. I miss Dad."

"I know, baby. I do, too," she whispers.

* * *

The ride home is long and silent. Jen doesn't say a word until we were almost to our exit. Then she starts off with, "Would you like to explain yourself? Why you ran off without telling us?"

"Nope, I really don't." It's the wrong thing to say, but I have a feeling that there is no right thing to say at the moment. When Jen bangs a fist on the steering wheel, I feel horrible. I've never seen her this mad. "Sorry," I mumble.

"What?"

"I said I'm sorry," I say a little louder. "I didn't think you'd care if I left. I mean, I heard you asking how much longer you have to keep me."

"That's not…ugh!" Jen swings the Suburban into the Chick-fil-A parking lot and throws the gear into park. "Did you hear the entire conversation, or did you just hear part of it and then make assumptions?"

80

I glare at her. "I heard enough. My mom is going to give up her parental rights, the Bartletts want to adopt my brothers, and Diane is going to try to find someone who will adopt me."

Jen closes her eyes and takes a deep breath. When she opens them again, she says slowly, "Did you hear the part where I said that if that happens, if your mom loses her parental rights, that Michael and I would love nothing more than to be your parents forever?"

The shock on my face answers her question.

"But it's your decision, not mine. You get to decide if our family is right for you. I promise we will not force you to be a part of it. We won't be mad, and we will still love you no matter what you decide, okay?"

My head barely moves up and down. "You—you want to be my mom?"

No words come out of her mouth. She wipes a tear from my cheek that I didn't know was there and nods her head. Her blue eyes are wet and shimmery, so colorful and different from mine. Her chin starts to quiver, and then she embraces me. "I love you," she whispers. "And don't you ever, ever scare me like that again!"

I'm still so shocked that I can't get anything to come out of my mouth. When Jen pulls back, she looks nervous. I'm sure she's wondering what I'm thinking about all of this, but I just need a minute to think.

"Oh!" she says, reaching for the glove compartment. "Look what I got." She pulls a manila envelope out and starts to open it. She pulls out a picture of me and grins. "I contacted the school and was able to get a copy of this to put in our picture frame in the kitchen."

"The one with the question mark," I say.

"If it's okay with you, of course."

I think about that the rest of the way home, imagining my face framed next to Brynn's and Brock's. Like I'm an actual part of the family. How would that feel? It doesn't take me long to figure out the answer to that question.

I know the second we drive up the steep driveway that I am in big, big trouble, because Diane is standing on the front porch with a sour expression on her face. It's okay, though, because, this time, I actually want to talk to her.

I step out of the car and walk right up to her. Right when she opens her mouth to scold me, I disarm her with a tight hug. "Can we talk in private?" I ask.

She stammers a second and then nods, pointing me to the front door, from which Michael, Brynn, and Brock burst out to smother me with affection.

"You're back! You're back!" Brynn squeals.

Jen shuffles them all to the kitchen, and I'm left alone with one confused and angry caseworker. She flops onto the easy chair and rubs her temples like I've given her the migraine of a lifetime. "What you did was very dangerous and irresponsible, Sefina."

"You're right," I say. "It was stupid. I heard you guys talking about my mom giving up her parental rights, and I got really mad, and I reacted like an idiot. I'm really sorry."

She opens one eye and looks at me, probably surprised that I'm not arguing with her like I usually do.

"I thought I could convince my mom to try harder, but after

seeing her and talking to Jen…"

Diane sits up and leans her elbows on her knees, listening.

I take a deep breath and release it, flopping down on the sofa in front of her. "I guess, for the first time in a long time, I feel like I'm going to be okay."

She nods, and the corner of her mouth quirks up.

"I want Jen and Michael to adopt me."

Diane fails to cover the surprise on her face, and maybe I have a little bit of the same surprise on my own face. But I know it's true. "They love me. I love them. They take good care of me. Plus, I know they'll let me see my brothers as often as possible."

"Wow," Diane says. "That's big. And that's fast. When did you come to this decision?"

"Today," I say. "I mean, I guess I knew it a while ago, but I didn't know it was an option. When Jen told me they want me…"

Diane tilts her head, waiting. I know she thinks my decision is too rash. Maybe it is, but I know in my heart that it's not going to change. "I thought about how when I was standing in front of Mom's rehab center, I was too scared to go in. Then Jen showed up. As soon as I saw her, I knew I'd made a huge mistake leaving her. I felt like everything was going to be okay because she was there. I want every day to feel like that, you know?"

She purses her lips and blinks her dull, doubtful eyes. "You just saw your mom, Sefina. It's an emotional day. You're probably feeling a little sad. Maybe you ought to give it some time."

"I will always feel sad about my parents," I say. "But like Jen told me when I first got here, there is no time limit on grief. It ebbs and flows as it pleases, but I'm willing to experience it all. I can be sad and happy at the same time."

For once, I was probably telling Diane what she wanted to hear, and it also happened to be the truth. And for the first time in forever, I felt like singing out of happiness.

CHAPTER

FOURTEEN

SEFINA

Chloe leans against the locker next to mine and twirls a strand of pink hair around her index finger. I'm not sure I like the new look on her, but she said she wanted something fresh to celebrate springtime. She sighs dramatically. I consider pretending like I don't notice, but I give in. "What's the problem now?" I ask.

"You never tell me anything, which I both love and hate about you. But I had to hear it through Colton that your mom signed away her rights yesterday."

I shrug. "Yeah? So? It's been in the works for months. We all knew it was going to happen."

"Yeah? So?" she mimics in a snotty tone. "But I didn't know when it would happen! That's kind of a big deal, sister! It's the kind of thing you should confide in me."

I snort and then shove my science book under all my other books. "Wait. You also love that I didn't tell you?"

She rolls her eyes and picks at her neon-green fingernail polish. "What I don't love is when people confide stupid things in me. They think that because I have a chunky butt, I will be understanding when they tell me they snarfed down an entire box of Girl Scout cookies. I can do without that kind of confession."

I shut the locker and turn to face her. "Nobody thinks you have a chunky butt, Chloe."

"I do," a female voice coos from behind me. Chloe's expression falls, and I turn to see Kasey Taggert, who's grinning like a toddler that just found sharp scissors.

"Shut up, Kasey," I say.

Her grin falls, and she steps closer to me so we are eye to eye. "Did you say something, foster freak?" The "k" in freak pops so loudly it makes my Samoan blood boil. I clench my fists and tense my muscles, knowing full well that I could pound her into the ground without suffering anything more than a delicate scratch from her perfectly manicured fingernails.

"She's not a foster freak!" a small voice yells to the side of me. I feel a small hand tug at my arm, and I do a double take when I look down and see Brynn, her eyes flaming with defiance.

"She's not a freak at all," Brock says, stepping to my other side. "She's our sister!"

Kasey lets out a surprised chuckle, but she steps back.

I pull the kids so they're facing me. "What are you guys doing here? It's the middle of the school day!"

90

Brynn points behind me. When I turn and see Jen standing there, wringing her hands, I know something is very, very wrong.

JEN

I am glad I waited until we were all piled into the Suburban before I tell Sefina about her grandmother, because her knee-jerk reaction is to scream at the top of her lungs. It scares the younger kids, and pretty soon, Brynn is in tears, too.

After several minutes, something changes in Sefina's posture. She sits up as if she is resolved to be strong.

"Your Auntie Beth is going to pull everything together for the funeral," I say.

"And my mom?" Sefina's voice is now eerily calm.

How much more can this girl handle? But how can I hide the truth from her that nobody has been able to find Natia to tell her the news? She didn't return to the rehab center after yesterday's hearing.

"She's out overdosing, right?"

I hold my breath, shocked. "I don't know where she—"

"Can we go to my tree?" she blurts out. Without waiting for an answer, she hops out the door and crosses the parking lot to the park next to her school.

I grab a bag of tissues, just in case, and wave the kids out of their seats. They follow me onto the pathway lined with newly green grass. There's a slight chill to the breeze, just enough to warrant a jacket. Still, the sun's warm rays make me eager to pull up the sleeves

91

and soak in some vitamin D.

Sefina, as expected, is sitting under her tree, staring up at the spring buds that seem ready to burst open at any moment. I direct Brynn and Brock to the playground, and they run off.

"I think I know when it happened," she says.

I kneel down next to her and wait.

"I was listening to the radio last night in my room, and out of nowhere, they played 'Cecilia.' That's her song. We would play it over and over while we danced in her kitchen. And then I felt… I mean, I thought last night that I felt someone…" She hugs herself and looks up at me. "Just like this, like her arms were around me."

I don't know what to say to that. And maybe I don't need to say anything. So, I scoot next to her and put my arm around her shoulder.

Sefina relaxes her body against my shoulder. "She would have loved you."

I nod. "I already love her. I mean, she has to have a fun personality to love that naughty song."

Sefina giggles, and after a few seconds, it turns into full-out laughter. She sits up, wiping the tears from her grinning cheeks. "I told her it was naughty! She said, 'Sometimes, naughty is nice.'"

I laugh, too. Then, hoping this is the right time, I say, "Sef, there's something else."

Her grin fades a bit.

I hesitate, hoping she won't be too upset. "We have a court date for the adoption."

Shock registers on her face. "Already? When?"

"The day after Memorial Day."

She looks away, and my heart sinks. Maybe this is a bad idea. Maybe she can never really form an attachment to us. Through no fault of her own, she's lost everything that has ever mattered to her. And now, selfishly, I'm proposing that she be my child and love me as a mother.

"Two months." Her voice is so quiet I think I might have imagined it. But then she turns around and claps her hands frantically. "You're going to be my mommy in two months!" She covers her mouth and squeaks, and then she lunges at me.

CHAPTER

FIFTEEN

SEFINA

Dr. Swenson jots down a note in my file. When she looks back up at me, her eyes are alien huge behind her thick glasses. Above her, the fluorescent light buzzes and flickers. Behind her, the clock ticks on the wall. She's waiting for me to answer a question, but I didn't hear what she asked because I am too busy trying to find a comfortable position on the new sofa. I keep sliding off the slick green cushions. There's no hole with stuffing coming out to pick at. There's nothing to look at except her.

"Could you repeat the question?" I say.

She lifts her chin. "I asked how is school going."

"Oh," I say, pulling my legs into crisscross position and sitting tall to keep from shifting off the couch. "It's fine. I caught up in English, so I have a solid C now. I have better grades in the rest of my classes. Oh! And I joined the choir, but we summer break is only a week away, so we're not doing anything but watching movies in that class."

"Any more harassing notes shoved into your locker?"

I can't help but smile at remembering how, a few days ago, Kasey was rambling some nonsense about how I was so obsessed with Colton but he'd never care about me, and then he walked right up to me, threw his arm around my shoulder, and kissed my cheek. Her face turned purple in an instant. "No." I laugh. "No more notes."

"Have you had any contact with your brothers since their adoption was finalized?"

I nod enthusiastically. "Yeah, we hang out every Friday night now. Usually, it's movie night at my house, but last week, my parents took us to the jump house."

"Your parents?" She smiles, almost smugly, which I try not to let annoy me. "That sounds fun. How about Natia? Have you had any contact with her?"

Ugh. She's just trying to get me upset now. "A little. I know she's back at the rehab center, and I guess she's doing okay after her relapse. She called the other day to say she was happy for me and the Andersons."

"And how are you feeling about the upcoming adoption?"

I feel like I'm the luckiest and unluckiest girl on earth. I feel like I'm giving up a huge part of my identity but also gaining a brand-new, happy life. I feel conflicted, like I'm betraying my biological family by giving up my name, but I want so badly to be an Anderson that I can taste it. All I say is, "I'm ready."

"I agree," she says. She closes file number 9.19.0302 and pulls her glasses off so that they dangle from the chain around her neck. "You are ready, Sefina. It has been a pleasure." She pushes her chair back toward her desk. "A true pleasure to work with you over the past couple of years."

I narrow my eyes. "Why does that sound so final?"

"Because you're done making monthly visits here. I'm always here if you need me, but your caseworker and I agree that you are doing well enough communicating with your foster...er...your adoptive mom that we can suspend our meetings for now."

I know it's rude, but I can't stop the huge grin that forms and the "Yes!" that escapes my mouth.

If Dr. Swenson takes offense, she doesn't show it. She just laughs and assures me she will be at the adoption finalization to help celebrate the big day.

JEN

"I've never seen anything like this," I tell Michael as we pull camping chairs out of the back of the Suburban. When Sefina told us she wanted to spend Memorial Day at her grandma's cemetery, I was confused, but now I understand. The entire memorial park is crawling with people, mostly Polynesian people who have brought flowers, candles, flags, trinkets, pictures, instruments, canopies, grills, food, and laughter. Before we can get our own chairs and cooler unloaded, Sefina has found her aunt and uncle, whom I recognize from the

99

funeral a few months back. Little cousins surround her, hanging off her arms like seaweed on driftwood.

Colton, who is still not my favorite person after he helped Sefina run off to Santaquin, helps me carry the cooler to where Sefina's family engulfs her. Then, like a magnet, they let go of her and swarm me, giving me the same greeting, as if we've always been family.

"It's so good to see you, Jen!" Sefina's Aunt Beth says as she squeezes me tight. "And tomorrow is the big day, no? Oh, bless your soul." She reaches out and grabs Colton by the arm. "Is this the boyfriend?" she asks me with one eyebrow raised. When I nod, she grins. "A bit skinny." She pats him on the cheek as he blushes. "I can take care of that. Come on, boy, let's fatten you up." And with that, she yanks him away to a table overflowing with shredded meats, rice, and various grilled vegetables. Brynn and Brock have already found their way to the desserts and are helping themselves, as are some of Sefina's younger cousins.

We spend the afternoon there, watching Sefina soak in her culture and love of her family. As the sun starts to set, candles are lit all around the cemetery. We sit near where Sefina's dad, grandma, and grandpa are buried, and listen to story after story about them. Sefina is glowing in the memories. She's never looked more beautiful or happy than she does at this moment, lit by a combination of candlelight and sunset. I'm not the only one who notices, either. Colton is staring at her like his every breath depends on each one she takes. I chuckle at the thought that as of tomorrow, I will have a daughter who is old enough to date.

"Oh, Fina, Fina!" Uncle Loto says, pointing to Sefina and

waving a ukulele toward her. "We have to sing Grandma's favorite song before we go."

She takes the ukulele and, to my astonishment, plucks out a few chords. Pretty soon, she has a slow rhythm going, and Loto begins to croon, "Cecilia, you're breaking my heart, you're shaking my confidence daily." Then, as if they've practiced this hundreds of times before, Sefina picks up the pace and sings along with him. "Oh, Cecilia, I'm down on my knees, I'm begging you please to come home."

Little by little, the whole group joins in, singing and clapping along to the beat. Brynn tries to sing the words even though she doesn't know any of them, and Brock dances away like nobody is watching. Michael and Colton are the only ones who aren't singing, but they clap along and laugh when Sefina plays a sour chord.

After the song is over, hugs are given, goodbyes are said, and Sefina blows a kiss to her grandparents' tombstone. We start to load up, and Sefina grabs my arm with both hands. "Can we please, please, pleeeease stop at one more place before Colton goes home?"

Twenty minutes later, we are in Riverton Cemetery, in front of a tombstone. The epitaph reads: "The Earth, the Earth has lost a gem, Heaven has gained a star, the angels saw it shining here and called it from afar. Reece Jacobs – beloved son and brother."

This cemetery has a much different feel to it. There are no flowers, no music, no family parties telling stories of their loved ones. Here, it is dark and cold except for this one spot where my tender-hearted girl sits cross-legged with a ukulele her uncle gave her and a battery-operated candle flickering in front of her. I swear the light grows brighter as she starts to play.

Colton falls to his knees next to her and sings, "I see trees of green, red roses, too. I see—" He chokes up.

Sefina plays a few measures more and then takes over for him. "I see them bloom for me and you, and I think to myself, what a wonderful world."

CHAPTER
SIXTEEN

SEFINA

I can hear Tane and Ku whisper-arguing in the courtroom benches behind me. I turn around to shush them, but Mrs. Bartlett has beaten me to it, smiling as she straightens Tane's tie and touches Ku's angry face. He relaxes a little, and when she pokes the spot where his dimple should be, he breaks out in a grin and the dimple emerges like magic. Suddenly, the polished wooden barrier between them and me seems so much deeper. They have a whole new life without me. I'm happy for them, truly, that they have a family who loves them and can make them smile. But, man, do I miss being the one to make Ku grin like that.

I spin my chair back toward the front of the courtroom. The judge's chair sits empty while we all wait around. Diane is leaning over, murmuring instructions to Jen and Michael to speak into the microphone so the court reporter can hear their answers. Jen keeps tugging at the hem of her skirt and looking back to me to make sure I'm okay or that I haven't run away; I'm not sure which. I'm also not sure why she's so nervous, but it's not helping me feel calm at all. Worse than that, Michael keeps rubbing his hand down his pant leg and smiling this weird, not-at-all-Michael smile and nodding at everything the caseworker says. What are they so worried about? Are they having second thoughts?

I spin my chair, taking in all of the people who have come to support me: my brothers, the Bartletts, Brock and Brynn, Chloe and her parents, Colton and his mother, who waves at me like we're old buds, Uncle Loto, Auntie Beth, and their five kids, and the empty seat where Mom should be.

"All rise," the bailiff says. Then he introduces the Honorable Judge Barbara Hopkins.

We all stand, and it feels like everyone is holding their breath until the judge sits in her chair and asks us to sit. Before long, the attorney's questions for Michael begin. Mostly, she asks about things she already knows, like his name, address, and employment. Then she says, "Please describe the relationship you have with Sefina."

Michael turns to me, tears welling in his eyes. He leans in toward the microphone, but he keeps his gaze on me. "Sefina is a gift. She filled a hole in our family, and every day I am grateful for her presence in my life. She is kind like Jen, a jokester like me, and a loyal sister to Brynn and Brock. She belongs with us. She is already part of our family. We are just here today to make it official." He reaches across the table in front of Jen, and I grab his hand. "I love you," he mouths, but I'm too choked up to respond.

The attorney pushes a stack of papers across the table to Michael. "You understand that by signing this agreement and consent to adopt that you are taking on the obligation to educate, support, and act as a natural parent to Sefina Anderson?"

It's the first time I have heard somebody speak my new name, and it gives me goosebumps.

"Yes," Michael replies.

"And you understand that once you sign this agreement, you cannot take it back? It's final."

"Yes, thank goodness," he says. Even the judge chuckles at that.

Jen gets more or less the same questions from the attorney. When she's asked about our relationship with me, she can barely keep her emotions under control. "I didn't expect to fall in love with Sefina like I have," she says. "Taking in a teenager who has a whole life of experience, who has bonded tremendously with her biological family, and suffered so much trauma…it wasn't my plan to keep her any longer than necessary. But the thing about Sefina is that she is composed of love. She radiates goodness, and it's infectious. I am honored that she would be willing to be a part of our family. I love her as a daughter, and I always will."

I lay my head on her shoulder and soak it all in.

"Miss Sefina," the judge says.

I sit up, startled.

"Do you wish to be a part of the Anderson family?"

I nod. "Yes, Your Honor."

"Are they good to you?"

"Yes."

"And you feel safe with them? Nurtured?"

"Yes."

The judge then tells Jen and Michael to stand and raise their right hands. She tells them that they are already under oath. "Do you solemnly swear to treat Sefina Anderson in all respects as your natural child? Will you share your lives with her? Help to mold her mind, nurture her body, and enrich her spirit? Will you never betray her trust, dampen her hopes, or discourage her dreams? And will you make this commitment willingly, to cherish Sefina Anderson all the days of your lives?"

Jen and Michael both say yes, and a shudder runs down my spine.

"Court is granting adoption. Congratulations," the judge says.

The room erupts in cheers and clapping, and we are invited to approach the judge and have our pictures taken with her.

Sefina Anderson. It's a perfect fit for me.

JEN

It is surreal to link arms with Natia and watch our daughter flirt with Colton as they try to decide on which flavor of shaved ice they'd like. Tane, Ku, Brock, and Brynn have already dug into theirs while the adults mingle in front of the playground. Michael is arm wrestling one of Sefina's cousins on a picnic blanket, with Uncle Loto cheering them both on.

"I'm sorry I didn't go to the hearing," Natia says. "I just couldn't handle that today."

I close my eyes and bite back a comment on how this day is about Sefina, not Natia.

"I know," I say, patting her arm. "It's okay."

She rests her head on my shoulder. "I'm going to miss her so much."

"We're not going anywhere," I assure her. "Sefina will always be your baby. But we want you to focus on taking care of you now."

"I will," she says. "It's time for me to start fresh. Maybe I'll get it right this time."

"You're going to be okay, Natia. We're all going to be okay now. She even rode over here in the car—the little car, not the Suburban. She didn't even think about it."

Natia laughs. "Well, that's progress. I know she'll be okay. She has a nice new family. Plus, she tells me she got a new mp3 player preloaded by that boy of hers."

I have to chuckle at this. "Yes, Colton. That kid is starting to grow on me."

Sefina ends up with a bright red flavor that stains her lips as she eats. She and Colton make their way back to the shade of Sefina's tree, which is gorgeously leafed out now. I cannot help but think of the first day I found her there, pouring her heart out in song. She was so crumpled and fragile. Now all I see is her vibrancy and joy for life—the way it should be, the way I will always remember my daughter.

THE END

Dear Reader,

I hope you have enjoyed reading my debut novella, Under the Foster Freak Tree. Please take a moment to post a review on Amazon and Goodreads. This is the best way for independent authors and authors with small publishers to gain exposure and help sales.

Thank you!

NOTE FROM THE AUTHOR

In an ideal world, all children would have strong, loving connections with stable parental figures. Every child involved with the foster care system has a unique experience. My goal in writing Sefina's story was to generate empathy, not to vilify parents who have been separated from their children. I wanted to show how even a strong family can fall apart after experiencing heartbreaking trauma.

ACKNOWLEDGEMENTS

Thank you to everyone who believed in this project and helped make it happen. Linda, Cindy, Leigh, Bri, Kelly, Bobbie-Jo, Crystal (x2), Brandi, Alison, and especially my husband, Mark and my parents, David and Cindy. Thank you for your invaluable input--I couldn't have done this without you.

DISCUSSION QUESTIONS

- Who, if anyone, is to blame for Sefina's problems?
- Do you think addictive painkillers should be legal?
- How does the life-cycle of the maple tree apply to Sefina's experiences?
- What is the symbolism of the worn-out couch in Dr. Swenson's office?
- How does Sefina experience the five stages of grief?
  1. Denial/Isolation
  2. Anger
  3. Bargaining
  4. Depression
  5. Acceptance
- How does Sefina change over the course of the story?
- Why do you think Kasey is unkind to Sefina?
- Why is it important for Jen to understand Sefina's culture and background?

Made in the USA
San Bernardino, CA
22 September 2018